Tusk Tusk

David McKee

RED FOX

A Red Fox Book
Published by Random House Children's Books, 20 Vauxhall Bridge Road, London SW1V 2SA.
A division of The Random House Group Ltd, London, Melbourne, Sydney, Auckland, Johannesburg and agencies throughout the world. First published by Andersen Press 1978. Sparrow edition 1983. Beaver edition 1987. Red Fox edition 1990.
This Red Fox edition 2001. Printed in Italy by Grafiche AZ, Verona
ISBN 0 09 930650 6

11 13 15 17 19 18 16 14 12 10

Once, all the elephants in the world were black

or white. They loved all creatures,

but they hated each other,

and each kept to his own side of the jungle.

One day the black elephants decided
to kill all the white elephants,

and the white ones decided to kill the black.

The peace-loving elephants from each side
went to live deep in the darkest jungle.

They were never seen again.

A battle began.

It went on…

and on, and on…

until all the elephants were dead.

For years no elephants were seen in the world.

Then, one day, the grandchildren of the peace-loving

elephants came out of the jungle. They were grey.

Since then the elephants have lived in peace.

But recently the little ears and the big ears

have been giving each other strange looks.

Other books by David McKee in Red Fox

Prince Peter and the Teddy Bear
Charlotte's Piggy Bank
Isabel's Noisy Tummy
Not Now, Bernard
Two Monsters
Mary's Secret
Elmer
Elmer Again
Elmer on Stilts
Elmer and Wilbur
Elmer in the Snow
Elmer and the Wind
Elmer and the Lost Teddy
Elmer and the Stranger